WHIRRR

To David Barneda:
Brilliant artist, inspiring friend, great guy
—A.R.

THIS IS A BORZOI BOOK PUBLISHED BY ALFRED A. KNOPF

Text copyright © 2010 by Aaron Reynolds
Illustrations copyright © 2010 by David Barneda

Visit us on the Web! www.randomhouse.com/kids

Educators and librarians, for a variety of teaching tools,
visit us at www.randomhouse.com/teachers

Library of Congress Cataloging-in-Publication Data
Reynolds, Aaron.
Snowbots / by Aaron Reynolds ; illustrated by David Barneda. — 1st ed.
p. cm.
Summary: Rhyming tale of a fun day young robots spend playing in new-fallen snow.
ISBN 978-0-375-85873-4 (trade) — ISBN 978-0-375-95873-1 (lib. bdg.)
[1. Robots—Fiction. 2. Snow—Fiction.] I. Barneda, David, ill. II. Title.
PZ8.3.R328Sno 2010
[E]—dc22
2009019299

The illustrations in this book were created using acrylics and color pencils.

MANUFACTURED IN MALAYSIA
October 2010
10 9 8 7 6 5 4 3 2 1
First Edition

SNOWBOTS

by Aaron Reynolds

illustrated by David Barneda

ALFRED A. KNOPF   New York

In sleep mode,
snoozing,
lying down,
in houses throughout Clackentown,
the citizens are unaware
of silver snowflakes in the air.

Morning comes,
alarm clocks beep,
switched off by those
who want more sleep.
Wiping rust out of their eyes,
robot children start to rise.

Into bed each snowbot goes,
Eskimo kiss on metal nose.
Drifting off, instead of sheep,
some count snowflakes in their sleep.
Others dream of winds that blow,
and hope tomorrow brings . . .

more snow!

Brush off fenders,
shine and clean.
Cereal with gasoline.
Set for school and on their way,
robots face another day.

Surprises in the scenery
send shocks to their machinery.
A snowy blanket drapes the town.
Bottley Grade School closes down!

A blizzard for the record books!
Snatching scarves from grappling hooks,
robots dash into the frost,
remote control completely lost.

Second grader Chip McSqueak,
first to clank up Scrapyard Peak,
trash-can lid clutched in his fist,
launches down into the mist.

Sledding,
racing,
without fears,
powered by rotating gears.

At the bottom, Chip is last . . .
bigger bots all steamrolled past.

His bitty sister, Clockentyne,
has different kinds of play in mind—
robot angels
on the ground,
wing nuts waving up and down.

Bots of every make and size
fill the chill with joyful cries.
Icy sculptures dot the lands,
thanks, in part,
to chainsaw hands.

By afternoon, great battles roar.
Supersonic snowballs soar!

Snowball forts.

And snowball tanks.

The bigger bots start to advance!
The smaller bots don't stand a chance,
till . . .
Chip deploys quick-firing gear.
His conquering team lets out a cheer!

Then—WHOOSH!—
a crushing wind-chill factor,
like a robot trash compactor,
blows and pierces hulls with ease,
shorting robot batteries.

Robot brain freeze sets in quick
as processors go click-click—STICK!
Shorted by the wintry blast
stand icy robots . . .
frozen fast!

Robot kids? Refrigerated.
Robot parents? ACTIVATED!

Metallic moms
and dads of chrome
tow their little robots home.

To warm up every part and piece,
there's cocoa spiked with axle grease.
Steaming mug meets clinking jaws.
Mmm . . .
Outer casing finally thaws.

A hot oil bath helps Chip relax,
his copper ducky squeaks and quacks.

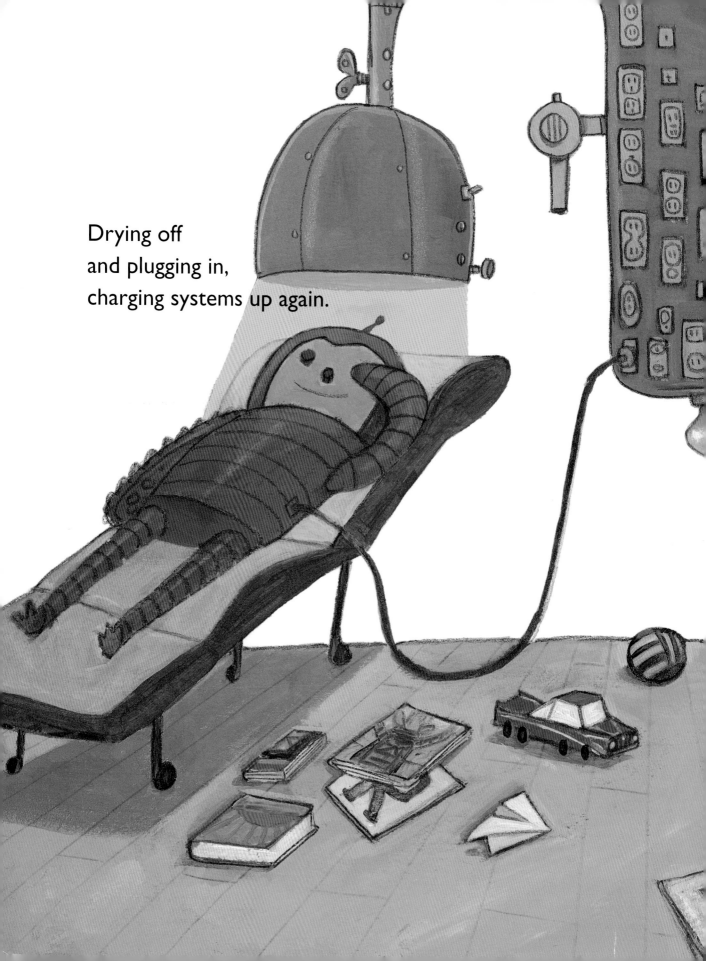

Drying off
and plugging in,
charging systems up again.

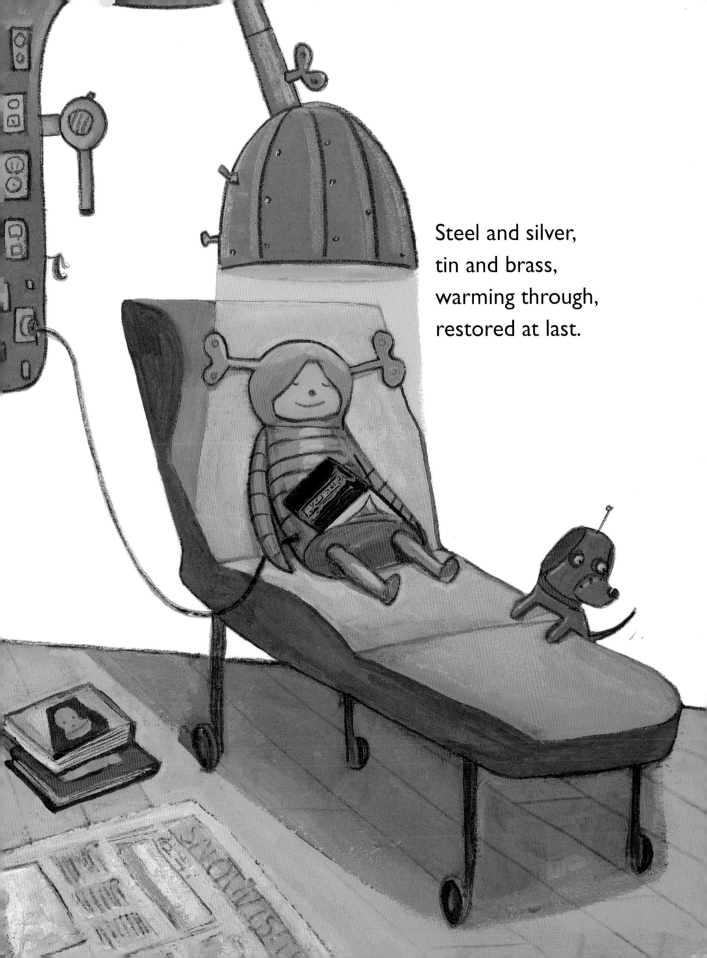

Steel and silver,
tin and brass,
warming through,
restored at last.